Marigold

and

the Feather of Hope, the Journey Begins

J. H. Sweet

Illustrated by Tara Larsen Chang

SOURCEBOOKS
Jabberwocky
AN IMPRINT OF SOURCEBOOKS

Published by Sourcebooks Jabberwocky, an imprint of
Sourcebooks, Inc.
P.O. Box 4410, Naperville, Illinois 60567-4410
(630) 961-3900
Fax: (630) 961-2168
www.sourcebooks.com

Library of Congress Cataloging-in-Publication Data

Sweet, J. H.
  Marigold and the Feather of Hope, the Journey Begins / J. H.
Sweet.
      p. cm.
  Summary: Spending two weeks with her eccentric aunt is not her
idea of fun, but nine-year-old Beth's attitude changes when she is
told that she and Aunt Evelyn are fairies and need to find the miss-
ing Feather of Hope.
  ISBN-13: 978-1-4022-0872-0
  ISBN-10: 1-4022-0872-3
  [1. Fairies—Fiction. 2. Friendship—Fiction. 3. Aunts—Fiction.] I.
Title.

PZ7.S9547Mar 2007
[Fic]—dc22
                                                            2006030307

Printed and bound in the United States of America.
          LB 10 9 8 7 6 5 4 3 2 1

To Ed,
for everything

MEET THE

Marigold

NAME:
Beth Parish

FAIRY NAME AND SPIRIT:
Marigold

WAND:
Pussy Willow Branch

GIFT:
Can ward off nasty insects

MENTOR:
Aunt Evelyn,
Madam Monarch

Dragonfly

NAME:
Jennifer Sommerset

FAIRY NAME AND SPIRIT:
Dragonfly

WAND:
Peacock Feather

GIFT:
Very fast and very agile

MENTOR:
Grandmother,
Madam Chrysanthemum

FAIRY TEAM

Thistle

NAME:
Grace Matthews

FAIRY NAME AND SPIRIT:
Thistle

WAND:
Porcupine Quill

GIFT:
**Fierce and wild in her
defense of others**

MENTOR:
Madam Robin

Firefly

NAME:
Lenox Hart

FAIRY NAME AND SPIRIT:
Firefly

WAND:
Single Piece of Straw

GIFT:
A great light within

MENTOR:
**Mrs. Pelter,
Madam June Beetle**

Inside you is the power to do anything

The Fairy Chronicles

Contents

Chapter One

Aunt Evelyn

Beth Parish sat on her living room sofa staring intently out of the large picture window that looked onto the driveway. While waiting for her aunt to pick her up, she was thinking about all the other things she'd rather be doing. Like any normal nine-year-old, Beth wanted to be reading, swimming, watching TV, playing video games, drawing, climbing trees in the back yard, or using her jewelry-making kit. Her mind was full of all of these things as she sat waiting, dreading spending two whole weeks with Aunt Evelyn.

Her suitcase was packed and ready by the door, but she was not able to take everything that she wanted. Beth's mother had only allowed her to pack a couple of books and her drawing pad with colored pencils, assuring her, "Aunt Evelyn will keep you very busy."

This was exactly what was troubling Beth. She hated the thought of weeding and kitchen work. She helped Aunt Evelyn with cooking, canning, and gardening every visit, but she had never been forced to spend two whole weeks there before.

Beth was on summer break from school and would rather be going to the pool every day, or playing with neighborhood friends, while waiting for summer camp to begin at the end of July. She sat sighing, staring, and twirling a lock of her curly golden brown hair with a finger. Dread settled in deeper and her dark brown eyes glazed over in boredom while she thought again about the fun things she'd rather be doing.

She had no time to ponder further as the crunch of car wheels in the driveway announced her aunt's arrival. Aunt Evelyn drove an especially old and ugly lime green station wagon. Beth hated riding in her car. It was terribly embarrassing with all the passersby giving them second looks. Why couldn't the car be like other old station wagons in dull colors of brown or tan? But Beth already knew the answer to this. Her aunt wasn't like anyone else, so her car couldn't be normal.

For years Beth had been a little afraid of her aunt and all of the strangeness surrounding her. In the last year or so, the fear had been replaced by annoyance. It seemed that Aunt Evelyn's favorite thing to do at the last several holiday dinners was watch Beth intently and follow her around, asking questions about school, friends, books, and

 4

her drawings. According to Beth's mother, Aunt Evelyn was just lonely and wanted to spend time with her favorite niece.

Mrs. Parish had the front door open and was motioning Beth to come get her suitcase. Aunt Evelyn hugged her sister then turned to Beth. "All ready, dear? Got everything packed?"

"I think so," Beth answered grudgingly.

Eyeing her aunt as she passed her with the suitcase, Beth thought there was something even stranger than usual about her today. It wasn't the clothes or shoes. Aunt Evelyn always wore oddly colored, loose-fitting dresses, brightly colored socks, and sneakers in strange colors. Today her sneakers were red, her dress turquoise blue with fringed sleeves, and her socks were bright yellow. She also wore an orange and black striped scarf draped over her shoulders.

Beth hoped they would be going straight to her aunt's house and not stopping anywhere on the way. She didn't want to be seen with anyone who dressed like this. Glancing at her aunt as she buckled her seat belt, Beth finally figured out what was different today. Aunt Evelyn seemed nervous.

Aunt Evelyn only lived about five miles across town. But it always took a very long time to travel the distance. Aunt Evelyn liked to drive back roads and byways. So instead of going the shortest route—straight down Court Street and through the town square—she turned left on McNeil, right on Washington, left on Pleasant Hill, then went through four stop signs before turning right on Wallace.

Beth scrunched down in the seat to avoid eye contact with the people turning to stare at the lime green car. Glancing sideways at her niece, Aunt Evelyn smiled and said, "She's not much to look at, but she runs good." Beth turned pink, feeling guilty that her aunt knew what she was thinking.

Turning onto Fig Circle, they were now in a quiet, older neighborhood. Beth couldn't figure out why her aunt had taken Fig Circle since there was no other outlet and they would be coming out right where they went in, but the answer soon became clear as the car slowed to a crawl. Enraptured by a beautiful garden in front of a large yellow house, Aunt Evelyn breathed, "Look at those zinnias, Bethy."

Aunt Evelyn loved flowers of all kinds. Beth had to admit they were very pretty. By the time they made the full circle and saw several other spectacular gardens, Beth was already planning to get her colored pencils out later to try to capture some of the flowers on paper. She didn't know that Aunt Evelyn had other ideas for their afternoon.

Finally, after six more turns, they arrived at Number Sixteen Cherry Lane. Aunt Evelyn's house was as colorful as her clothes and car. The frame house was

painted robin's egg blue with tangerine trim. The shutters were bright canary yellow and matched the wooden picket fence bordering her front garden. The front door was apple red, and her porch swing was a grassy green color. Beth had never seen so many mixed-up colors that didn't go together. She could only assume that her aunt bought paint whenever she found it on sale, or used leftovers from friends, and didn't care whether the colors matched or even looked good.

Beth lugged her suitcase up the porch steps and upstairs to the guest room. Even though this room had colors as mixed up as everywhere else in the house, Beth was very comfortable here. The bumpy, dark blue bedspread was soft, and the pale pink sheets always smelled like fabric softener. An old smooth pecan dresser, oak rocking chair, and antique brass floor lamp completed the furnishings. On the dresser sat a bowl of acorns.

Beth smiled at the new throw pillows in the rocker: one was green plaid and the other was red with dark purple trim. It suddenly occurred to Beth that her aunt must be colorblind. She had heard about colorblindness on television, and it was certainly a good explanation for her aunt's odd tastes.

After putting her clothes in the dresser and closet, Beth wandered downstairs. Her aunt was in the kitchen and greeted her with a lopsided smile. "All unpacked, dear? Have a seat so we can talk." Aunt Evelyn gestured to the round table with four chairs in the kitchen bay window.

Beth climbed onto the nearest tall wooden chair. It was smooth and cool, and there was a pleasant breeze wafting down from the ceiling fan above her. Aunt Evelyn meanwhile was

digging in the refrigerator. "Ah, root beer. It got pushed to the back."

Beth was very pleased and surprised. Evidently at the last few holiday visits, her aunt had noticed that Beth liked root beer.

This was a very nice change from last summer when Aunt Evelyn seemed to chase her around every day with tea and cookies. Looking more nervous than ever, Aunt Evelyn sat down next to Beth and popped the tops of two root beers, carefully placing them on coasters.

After several swigs, squinted eyes, a smack of her lips, and a comment of, "I believe I'd rather have tea," Aunt Evelyn stared at her niece through her little tortoiseshell horn-rimmed glasses. Beth looked back at

her aunt uneasily. She jumped a little when Aunt Evelyn exclaimed, "Okay! Ask me anything you like. You must have a million questions."

Beth stared at her aunt, wondering what she was supposed to ask about. Several polite questions did pop into her mind including, *What's that new little pink flower by the front steps? What happened to the old pillows that used to be in the rocker upstairs? Is it okay to spread my drawing pencils and paper out on the coffee table this afternoon?*

She never got to ask any of these questions because her aunt suddenly remembered, "Oh, that's right, I haven't told you yet. I've just been rehearsing this for ages, so it seems like I already told you."

Somewhat alarmed, Beth slid sideways in her seat putting about a foot of extra distance between her and her aunt. Aunt Evelyn was leaning forward, obviously very excited about something. Her dark brown eyes, now flashing with flecks of orange and black, were a bit scary. Beth had never seen these colors in her aunt's eyes before. Noticing that Beth was cringing, her aunt sat back a little, slightly more relaxed. They both took a deep breath, staring at each other as the room became very still.

Beth felt a tingling sensation, as though something very important was about to happen. Aunt Evelyn continued to stare at her. Just as Beth was thinking of having another sip of soda, her aunt stated calmly, "You are a marigold fairy."

Chapter Two

Marigold Fairy

For a few moments, they just looked at each other. Aunt Evelyn was watching her expectantly, and Beth was thinking, *This woman is crazy! How can Mom and Dad leave me for two whole weeks with a crazy woman?*

Aunt Evelyn seemed to sense that she had not quite gotten her point across, so she tried again. "Let's start over." She paused, lowering her voice, and said very slowly, "You… are…a…fairy." She emphasized each word, leaving out the marigold this time.

As if that made any difference! Beth was starting to get a little panicky. How was a nine-year-old supposed to deal with a crazy woman? She no longer cared that Aunt Evelyn knew her car was ugly, or that she figured out Beth liked root beer. None of that mattered because her aunt was a lunatic. Beth frantically thought, *I'll just nod along, then when she leaves the room, I'll call home.* This seemed like the best plan. But it was easier said than done. Aunt Evelyn was looking even more closely at her.

"You've had a bit of a shock, dear." Sliding a plate towards Beth, she added, "Have a cookie."

"Um…Um…I…" That was as far as she got. Beth, who was usually a chatterbox, could think of nothing else to say.

Her aunt was now smiling and looking at her kindly. She left the table and began busying herself with making tea. Looking over at the table, Aunt Evelyn said, "I wanted to tell you earlier, but you weren't quite old enough. I am a fairy too, a monarch butterfly fairy. I'll show you in a little while so you'll believe me."

She glanced over at Beth, who looked dazed, and who now had a cookie in each hand but had not taken a bite. Aunt Evelyn continued in a breezy voice. "I know you think I'm crazy, but you'll soon see."

The tea was ready and Beth watched as her aunt floated into the living room. Suddenly, phoning home seemed rather silly. After all, Aunt Evelyn didn't seem dangerous, just loopy. She couldn't think of anything else to do, so putting down the cookies, she slid out of her chair and followed her aunt into the living room, carrying her root beer and a coaster with her.

A few minutes later, sitting on the sofa and sipping root beer, Beth was pulled out of deep thought by her aunt's voice. "Are you ready for me to show you?" Unable to think of anything to say, Beth gave a small nod.

The transformation of Aunt Evelyn into a fairy happened very quickly with a small *pop*. In fact, Beth thought she just disappeared. "Here I am, dear," uttered a tiny voice. As Beth looked closely at the armchair her aunt had occupied, she saw a small figure standing beside the green throw pillow.

Beth leaned forward to see her aunt more closely. She was still Aunt Evelyn, but was more beautiful than anything Beth could have imagined. She still had short, wavy, dark brown hair, but now there was a small crown of golden flowers perched on top. Delicate orange and black butterfly wings extended out of her shoulders. Her gauzy fairy dress fell almost to her ankles and was subtle shades of orange, brown, gold, and black. She had a belt of a fawn tan color and soft slippers to match.

Beth was mesmerized as her aunt took flight, circled the room twice, and came to land back in the armchair. With another small *pop* Aunt Evelyn was again sitting in the chair reaching for her teacup. "Now, let's talk a little before you take fairy form," she said. "The reason you can see me as a fairy is because you know I'm a fairy, and because you *now* know that you are a fairy yourself.

"When regular people see me, they see a monarch butterfly. You have seen me as a butterfly, before you knew that you were a fairy. I attended some tea parties in your back yard with your dolls and friends. But you probably don't remember because you were very young. By the way, that's why I always thought you liked tea, because of the tea parties. It's been a long time since I was a little girl; I forgot that tea parties have nothing to do with liking tea."

Her aunt laughed, then continued. "Now, you have to be careful about being seen by regular people, even though they will only see you as a marigold flower. Marigolds don't often bloom in winter, so

 20

you have to limit your fairy activities that time of year. And you have to be especially careful of flying because people will think it odd to see a marigold flying through the air, unless it's a very windy day. I think you should limit your outdoor flying to night-time and foggy days for now. We'll do our practicing indoors.

"I have to be careful when flying around too. Old Mrs. Hannigan, two doors down, nearly netted me last summer. Nice lady, keeps a butterfly journal. She was chasing after me, yelling and screaming that monarch butterflies are never seen here in July. I just barely got away. Needless to say, I now take a different route when I leave."

Beth listened carefully to everything her aunt was telling her, but she was still in a bit of shock, and she wasn't sure she really believed it all. Aunt Evelyn seemed to sense this because she stated, "You'll start believing all of this as soon as you see your fairy self."

Deciding it was time to speak, Beth asked, "Am I still human?"

Her aunt seemed to find this amusing and laughed heartily, answering, "Of course, dear. You are still human and you still have a soul. But you also have a fairy spirit. Yours is a marigold flower, and you have a special gift relating to that particular fairy spirit, but we will get to that later. Are you ready to take fairy form?"

 22

Beth nodded as her aunt proceeded to instruct her. "Move about a foot to the left dear. Standard fairy form is six inches, and I don't want to lose you in the crack between the sofa cushions. Fairies can be different sizes, but that will take some learning, and it's not always safe. What would people think if they saw a six-foot butterfly or a ten-foot flower? No, no, we'll leave all the complicated stuff till later."

Beth slid over as her aunt went on. "You are already a fairy, so this will actually be very easy. Close your eyes the first time because it's a bit of a rush and I don't want you to get dizzy. Just imagine that you *are* your fairy self." Beth did as she was told and imagined herself as a tiny marigold flower with wings. Instantly, there was a small *pop*.

For a moment, Beth thought something went wrong because her aunt exclaimed, "Oh dear, I forgot!" But as Beth opened

her eyes, she was sitting perched on the edge of the couch with a giant Aunt Evelyn smiling down at her, saying, "No, nothing's wrong dear. You are perfect. I just forgot the mirror. Don't try to fly yet." Aunt Evelyn rushed out of the room and returned a few seconds later with a large hand mirror, which she propped against one arm of the couch.

Beth got up and walked over to the mirror for the first view of her fairy self. She had a crown of tiny yellow marigold flowers and feathery pale gold wings, in a smaller size than Aunt Evelyn's wings. Her fairy dress came to just above her knees and seemed to be made of yellow and gold crinkly marigold petals in a sort of overlapping striped pattern. She had the same fawn belt and slippers as her aunt. The crown of flowers contrasted beautifully with the golden brown curls on her head, and the petals of her wispy dress shone like the sun. Beth, who never cared much for her looks before, had to admit she was a beautiful fairy.

Aunt Evelyn landed beside her with a small *whoosh*, taking her hand and saying, "Now we're going to fly. Go on, try your wings." Beth looked over her shoulder and tried to move her wings. Just by thought, her wings began moving very fast, in whispery waves that tickled her ears, and she was lifted several inches off the sofa, her aunt beside her. She then concentrated on slowing her wings and landed with a slight bounce.

"Good job!" exclaimed her aunt. "Now we'll try going around the room." They lifted off, still holding hands and circled the room three times. "Just imagine a nice soft landing," Aunt Evelyn instructed, and they floated down, landing gently on the sofa. Beth, excited and proud, was all smiles as her aunt hugged her tightly.

Chapter Three

Fairy Things

They practiced flying for the next fifteen minutes or so. Then they sat down together for a rest on a pink throw pillow.

"Next we'll have a look at your wand," Aunt Evelyn told Beth. "I've been keeping it for you. You're going to love it. All you have to do is call for it. Some fairies like to carry their pixie sticks around with them in their belts. But you don't have to. It will come when you call. Just hold out your hand and call for it."

A little tentatively Beth held out her hand and said questioningly, "Here wand?" Instantly, she was clutching a tiny, beautiful pussy willow branch. The soft pussy toes, which Aunt Evelyn explained were blooms, gleamed a creamy golden color against the dark brown of the branch. As Beth lightly stroked one of the soft blooms, the whole wand quivered and purred.

"It's an enchanted pussy willow stem; I thought you would like it. There are many types of fairy wands," Aunt Evelyn explained. "Mine is a single dandelion seed." As she spoke, the gleaming dandelion seed wand appeared in her hand. "By the way, you can call for it and put it away without words, just by thought. It's part of the enchantment." Beth thought of putting away her wand and was pleasantly surprised when it disappeared. Then she thought of holding it again, and actually laughed with delight to find it immedi-ately softly purring in her hand.

"No wand tricks just yet, dear," Aunt Evelyn said. "We will want to talk about your fairy handbook first."

Beth didn't have a chance to ask what a fairy handbook was. Instead, she froze with fear as Aunt Evelyn's orange cat, Maximillion, bounded into the room and looked straight at them with his yellow eyes. Aunt Evelyn smiled reassuringly and said, "Don't worry, Bethy, he won't hurt you. Most animals like fairies. In fact, in fairy form, you can talk to animals. Go on, say something to him."

Beth cleared her throat and started with, "Um...hi, Maxim." The cat blinked and continued to stare.

"Well, he's not going to talk back," said Aunt Evelyn. "Animals can't talk unless they're bewitched. They communicate in other ways. Ask him to do something for you."

"Um...Maxim, would you please bring me the towel by the sink in the kitchen?" Maximillion was out of the room and back with the dishtowel so quickly that Beth was shocked. "Thank you," she added, laughing as he lightly rubbed his head against her shoulder. He seemed fully aware that she was only six inches high and was very gentle in touching her. He purred like her wand, only stronger, then crossed the room and jumped into a comfortable lilac armchair, curling into a ball and settling in for a nap.

"Where were we?" Aunt Evelyn asked. "Oh yes, the handbook." From out of thin air, a tiny book appeared. It was a fawn color like her slippers, very soft, and had gold lettering on it. Beth read the gleaming words, *First Fairy Handbook.* Then her aunt produced a second book, adding, "This is mine." Beth glanced at it and read the words, *Formidable*

Fairy Handbook. At Beth's questioning look, her aunt smiled and explained, "Yes, I'm very formidable at this age.

"You see, the handbook ages with you Beth. Right now it is full of information and answers to questions that a nine-year-old will understand. When you get a little older it will change to the *Fortunate Fairy Handbook*. For some reason, fairies around ages ten to twelve are very reckless and accident-prone, and get into trouble easily. The *Fortunate Fairy Handbook* will help you out of pickles and jams when this happens. It knows to be extra diligent and careful with information and answers during this time.

"The explanations and instructions in the book will become more complex and detailed as you get older and need more information. I just read twenty-two pages on a subject that had a one-sentence answer when I was your age. But you won't be able to read *my* book," Aunt Evelyn added shrewdly, handing it to her. Beth was amazed that the word *Formidable* immediately changed to *First* when Beth's fingers touched the book. "For safety reasons," her aunt said consolingly but sternly. "There are some things you do not need to know yet and should not attempt until you are much older."

Aunt Evelyn went on to explain that future handbooks would include *Fanciful*, for the teen and early adult years; *Formidable*, for the years in which fairies are capable of taking most matters entirely in hand by themselves, making few mistakes; and *Final*, for the most accomplished and oldest fairies, who never really need advice, but read the handbook mainly out of sentiment or forgetfulness.

"I've been *Formidable* for twenty-six years now!" Aunt Evelyn exclaimed proudly. "Those are pretty much the main categories unless you're doing something very wrong, then it is likely to say *Foul*.

 32

"My friend, Patsy Wingate, told me that hers said *Fair Fairy Handbook* for a whole month once when she was thirteen. But it was during a time when she was cheating on her spelling tests at school. She started getting a lot of unasked-for messages from the handbook whenever she would look things up: messages about fair play, integrity, not taking an easy route, and the importance of education. As soon as she stopped cheating, the book became *Fanciful* again. A handbook might also be labeled *Foolish* if a fairy becomes too careless or silly. There are a few others, but those are the most common."

Aunt Evelyn evidently decided they had done enough fairy things for one day because she said, "Now keep yourself busy this afternoon while I do some chores. After dinner, I'll tell you where we are going tomorrow."

While Aunt Evelyn went to put a load of laundry in the washer, Beth busied herself

Fairies

Delightful, magical
spirits with like-
nesses & kinship
to flowers, insects,
& other small
creatures. Fairies
are problem solvers,
helpers, fixers, &
protectors of nature...

34

looking up information in her handbook. It was organized alphabetically, just like a dictionary. She first looked up the word *fairies* and read the handbook's entry.

Fairies: Delightful, magical spirits with likenesses and kinship to flowers, insects, and other small creatures. Fairies are problem solvers, helpers, fixers, and protectors of nature. They get along well with gnomes and most other living things.

Aloud, Beth repeated the words "delightful, magical spirits," smiling at the brilliant description of her newly discovered fairy self. She then looked up *gnomes*.

Gnomes: Earth spirits who make flowers, plants, trees, crystals, and minerals grow. They add colors to nature and work with fairies to ensure the protection of earth's treasures. Gnomes have the ability to disguise themselves so they can go about their business undetected. To regular humans, a gnome will look like an ordinary object such as a tree stump, a watering can, or an acorn squash.

Remembering what Aunt Evelyn said about fairy size, Beth looked up the word *size* and was surprised when the handbook addressed her personally.

Beth (Marigold): Standard fairy size is six inches. You are not ready to learn how to be any other fairy size. However, here is a hint for the future: to be larger, you will need a bit of asparagus. To be smaller, you will need a bit of radish.

 36

Beth laughed. Wondering what other advice she might be given, she looked up the word *wand*.

Beth (Marigold): Your wand is a pussy willow stem or branch, enchanted to help you perform fairy magic. It will purr when happy and scratch when upset. You are not yet ready for fancy wand tricks. However, look up "fairy light."

Beth did as the handbook said.

Fairy Light: *Fairy light is a* **whisper of light for your eyes to hear.** *The tip of your wand will glow. This is a useful tool for fairies. To produce this light, you must whisper the words* **"Fairy light."**

After softly whispering, "*Fairy light,*" the tip of her wand did indeed glow softly. Beth smiled to herself, delighted to have learned her first wand trick.

Beth spent the rest of the afternoon looking up information and getting answers to her questions. Then, after a wonderful dinner of pepperoni pizza and salad, Aunt Evelyn said, "Tomorrow we are going to a Fairy Circle. You will get to meet a lot of other fairies and hear what is going on in the fairy realm. I don't want you to ask any more questions tonight. I think you have had quite enough to digest for one day."

After watching television for an hour, Beth wandered sleepily up to her room. Before going to bed, she looked up one more handbook entry.

Fairy Circle: A gathering of fairies that can be for social reasons or to discuss problems. To clear up any

confusion, please note that Fairy Circles do not have to be circular. Fairies can meet together in any shape or formation including squares, triangles, straight lines, untidy clumps, scattered groups, piled pyramids, hovering clouds, etc. Some reasons that may necessitate a Fairy Circle include natural disasters, important news, major problems, or fairy celebrations.

Beth went to sleep quickly and dreamed of meeting other fairies.

Chapter Four

Fairy Circle

hey set off after breakfast in the lime green car, which Beth now thought was pretty cool. The color didn't bother her anymore. She even waved at one onlooker, rather than cringing with embarrassment. Beth was on her way to a Fairy Circle to meet other fairies, and she couldn't be happier.

For some reason, Aunt Evelyn was rather thoughtful and subdued. They had been driving about twenty minutes when she spoke. "Beth, sometimes we have to meet to discuss bad things that are happening."

Beth answered cheerfully, "I know. Fairies need to meet to discuss problems and ways to fix them. Fairies are fixers. I looked it up in my handbook."

"That's a good attitude," her aunt replied. "It shows that you already have some understanding of the responsibility of being a fairy."

While she drove, Aunt Evelyn told her, "Fairy spirits are created by Mother Nature. She is the fairy guardian."

"Will I get to meet Mother Nature?" Beth asked.

"Oh, no!" Aunt Evelyn exclaimed. "No, no, no. Very few fairies ever meet her. She is too busy, very powerful, and often dangerous. We can't take a chance that she won't be in lightning or tornado form rather than something safe like mist, echo, or drizzle. Fairies are only a very small part of a much larger whole. We must be content to do our jobs as a part of this plan, without necessarily understanding all of it." Beth sat thinking this over, without asking any more questions.

They turned down a gravelly country road, which was narrow and winding. The trees grew dense, branches sometimes scraping the sides of the car. Soon they turned into a clearing where several other oddly colored cars were parked. Aunt Evelyn told Beth, "Some fairies are flying in, but it's a bit of a stretch for us since you haven't flown much yet." They walked quietly along a path through the clearing.

Beth thought they were going to enter the woods, but they stopped just short of a large weeping willow tree at the far edge of the clearing. Hundreds of long, leafy tendrils brushed the ground, and the breeze blowing through them sounded like soft windy music.

"Here we are," said Aunt Evelyn. "Do you know why we are meeting under a willow

tree?" When Beth shook her head, her aunt answered, "Because willow trees inspire communication and creative ideas, and today we have a very important problem to discuss."

Aunt Evelyn continued, "We meet under oak trees when we seek wisdom about important plans for the future. Oak trees are very wise and full of vision. Of course, we specifically look for younger oak trees, a hundred years or less, because older oaks do not give up their wisdom easily. They are so full of knowledge and mystery that they often choose not to share information. When old oaks do agree to share their knowledge, it is usually given to us in riddles that are so clever, they can seldom be worked out quickly enough to be of use to anyone."

As a final note on the subject of trees, Aunt Evelyn added, "And we sometimes meet under apple trees when we need advice from unicorns. Unicorns are drawn to apple trees, and their advice is very valuable. They have a purity of spirit and a clarity of thought that is always of a selfless and unbiased nature, with no ulterior motives or prejudices to cloud the issues." As Beth pondered this, her aunt said, "Well, in we go, time to meet other fairies."

They transformed into their fairy selves and walked through the swinging willow branches. The sunlight grew dim as they approached the trunk. Beth paused, transfixed by her first sight of so many other fairies. Aunt Evelyn stopped just outside of the main group to allow her mesmerized niece to take it all in for the first time.

So far there were about twenty other fairies at Fairy Circle. Some were obviously flower spirits. Her eyes wide with awe, Beth saw many flowers she recognized including a peach-colored rose, a red zinnia, a white lily, and a beautiful pale purple thistle fairy with straight blonde hair and spindly, pale gray wings.

She saw a yellow butterfly fairy whose wings were not as large and impressive as Aunt Evelyn's, but who was so bright it was almost like looking at the sun. There were

more butterflies and a few other insect fairies. An older, rather hearty June beetle fairy was buzzing around arranging stones and sticks in spots convenient for small groups to sit.

When Beth first saw the red dragonfly fairy, she couldn't take her eyes off her. Dragonfly was a thin, athletic black girl with extremely short hair combed into tiny waves very close to her head. Her dress and wings were a deep, dark blood red color. And when she moved, it was with a grace and power that commanded attention and inspired confidence. If Beth had to guess, she would have thought Dragonfly was a model, or maybe a professional athlete.

Beth was only able to drag her eyes away from Dragonfly when distracted by a flash of light. As she looked over, Beth saw a glowing, golden brown fairy. The firefly fairy winked and smiled at Beth, walking towards her.

Aunt Evelyn began introductions as several fairies approached. "Beth, this is Lenox Hart, or Firefly." They shook hands and Beth felt a rush of warmth that was almost as wonderful as the glowing vision of her new friend. Thistle's name was Grace Matthews. She had enormous gray eyes that matched the cloudy gray color of her wings, and her short blonde hair was spiky like the thistle petals of her dress and her pointy wings. Her handshake prickled slightly. Jennifer Sommerset was the dragonfly fairy Beth had admired. She shook hands with Beth in a vibrating, tickly sort of way. Thistle, Dragonfly, and Firefly seemed to be about the same age as Beth.

"Lenox is a very pretty name," Beth said shyly to Firefly.

"I'm named after my mom's china," Firefly answered. "Mom told me I was very pale when I was born, but I had a kind of shine, so she named me after her dishes."

Promising to be back shortly, Aunt Evelyn told Beth that she needed to talk to someone and walked off. Beth happily visited with her new friends, occasionally meeting other fairies who came over to them. Many were older and did not stay to visit, obviously preferring to keep company with those closer in age. Beth didn't mind. She was perfectly content to visit with Thistle, Dragonfly, and Firefly. They were very interested in her wand. "No one else has a pussy willow wand," Firefly told her. They passed it around, petting it, and giggling as the wand purred.

Thistle's wand was a porcupine quill. "I used to have a piece of braided horse hair—from the tail, you know," she said. "But it was too powerful for me—too much horse enchantment. It nearly shook my arm off. So I got permission to switch. This one fits my personality better anyway," she added happily, jabbing into the air with the sharp pointy quill. Dragonfly had a peacock feather wand, and Firefly's was a single gleaming piece of golden straw. They seemed to fit perfectly with the personalities of each fairy.

Beth noticed that the other girls called her *either* Marigold or Beth. For now, Beth was going to use their fairy names. Meeting so many new fairies at one time, she was afraid of mixing them up.

Aunt Evelyn was talking to the June beetle fairy. Firefly explained, "Madam June Beetle is my neighbor, Mrs. Pelter. She's my fairy mentor, like your aunt." She pointed out a yellow chrysanthemum fairy that was Dragonfly's grandmother and mentor. Then Firefly told her, "All the young fairies have mentors. But not all mentors are fairies. Thistle's mentor is that robin over there. Madam Robin is very old and wise. And she can talk, so she must have been bewitched somewhere along the line, which is very rare."

Beth thought she saw Madam Robin look sharply at them, as though she knew she was being discussed. This was confirmed when Firefly noticed the attention of the bird, turned pink, and added, "Oh, and robins hear very well too." With a slight flutter of her wing, Madam Robin turned tail and looked the other way.

Aunt Evelyn returned to their little group, bringing refreshments. They ate

mounds of tiny scrumptious powdered sugar puff pastries, while drinking sweet dewy nectar from real honeysuckle blossoms. They also had raspberries and homemade fudge.

A leafy fairy with tiny blue flowers scattered over her green dress stopped by to introduce herself. "I'm Spiderwort," she said. After a pause, she added wearily, "It's an herb," as though tired of having to explain. "Rosemary is here somewhere. She has blue flowers too. I think we are the only two herb fairies." Rosemary waved at them from across the gathering as she saw Spiderwort point to her.

While they continued to enjoy the refreshments, Aunt Evelyn gave Beth a small pouch full of glittering pixie dust. "You can tie this to your belt," her aunt explained. "We use pixie dust to help us perform magic."

Aunt Evelyn sat down next to Beth and told her, "Before the meeting begins, I want to tell you about your special gift as a marigold fairy." Firefly, Thistle, and Dragonfly all sat quietly and listened as Aunt Evelyn went on. "Each fairy has a special gift relating to her fairy spirit. For example, Jennifer's dragonfly spirit is very fast and agile. This coordination and speed helps her tremendously."

Dragonfly laughed and said, "Especially when I'm playing soccer."

"Rather an unfair advantage for friendly competition," said Thistle.

"Oh and you never use your gifts to your advantage, Thistle?" Dragonfly replied.

When Thistle didn't answer, Aunt Evelyn continued. "Grace has two gifts. The thistle is a very beautiful wildflower. She can attract, or distract, with her beauty if needed, but she can also ward off unwanted advances with her prickles. She has a wild fierceness that helps defend against attack.

"Lenox's firefly spirit holds a light greater than any other fairy. This is very useful in dark places and helps her to find her way. It is unlikely that she will ever get lost, because her light can lead her. And it also keeps her from being misguided by bad spirits."

Aunt Evelyn looked at Beth closely before going on. "Can you think of what your gift might be?" Beth couldn't think of what was special about a marigold flower and ended up shaking her head. Her aunt then asked, "Why does your mom plant marigolds in her vegetable garden?"

Beth thought for a few moments, then smiled happily, having finally worked it out. She told the others, "My mom plants marigolds all over her garden to keep bugs from eating the vegetables. Marigold flowers are natural bug repellents, kind of like citronella plants."

Aunt Evelyn nodded and went on. "So in addition to solving the mystery of why you have never been bothered by mosquitoes and chiggers like the rest of us, you have discovered your very useful and powerful gift. You have the ability to ward off insects. This will come in handy if you are ever faced with an unfriendly spider, locust, or hornet. Not all insects are friendly like butterflies, fireflies, and dragonflies.

"But you should never use your abilities lightly. Younger fairies are not allowed to use their gifts, or fairy magic, unless supervised by a fairy mentor. It will take some time to develop the wisdom and maturity needed to understand how to use your power properly. We must never misuse our gifts. They are given to us for specific purposes, to protect nature and fix problems. With this power comes responsibility. We are not allowed to use fairy magic to solve everyday problems or to abuse others."

Beth had a lot to think about after this lesson. She sat quietly and watched as Thistle and Dragonfly started swinging on the willow branches nearby.

Chapter Five

The Feather of Hope

*S*oon all of the fairies had arrived, and they moved closer to the center of the gathering. Beth noticed for the first time what looked like the leader of the group, a very old fairy that was unmistakably a toad. Madam Toad, in fact. Beth couldn't help staring at her. In contrast to all of the bright flowers and delicate insects, a toad fairy looked out of place.

Slightly wrinkled with age, Madam Toad was a muddy greenish-brown color, with small, dark green wings perched on her plump shoulders. When she spoke, there was no question of authority. Her voice was rich, loud, and very decisive, commanding immediate attention. "Welcome, welcome! Gather round and make yourselves comfortable. We have important business to discuss today. First of all, we need to welcome Marigold to our circle. Please make her feel at home and introduce yourselves later if you haven't already."

Beth moved forward with her aunt and the other fairies. Some stood, while others took the seats that Madam June Beetle had thoughtfully arranged. Beth sat on a smooth stone with her aunt, while her new friends sat on small branches and toadstools nearby.

Madam Toad waited until they had settled themselves before continuing. "We need a little extra light, I think." She produced her wand, which was a tiny miniature red rosebud stem, and used it to ignite a fire in a small pile of twigs and leaves in front of her. Firefly rose to the occasion, and with a wink to her friends, increased her glow by

double. On the other side of the group, a delicate tulip fairy placed her long crystal wand on a high toadstool, where it sat shimmering softly with light. And several other fairies whispered, "*Fairy light*," to set their wands aglow.

Dragonfly was scowling at the fire that Madam Toad had lit, looking very mad. But Beth didn't have time to wonder why Dragonfly was angry because Madam Toad started speaking again. "We have a guest speaker today. This is Brownie Christopher."

With this introduction, a small brownie stepped from the shadows behind Madam Toad. He had straight dark hair and was dressed in tattered, shabby, tan clothes. He wore an acorn cap as a hat, and on his face he wore an expression that looked like he'd rather be anywhere else than a Fairy Circle. Looking sullenly around, he fingered a slingshot and a small leather pouch on his belt, shuffling his feet and kicking at a twig.

At first there was silence from the group. Then mutterings began, followed by low buzzing conversations. "What's wrong?" Beth asked.

"Look up *brownie* in your handbook," Aunt Evelyn instructed quietly. Beth flipped the pages quickly.

Brownies: Small mischievous boy fairy folk who are generally seven inches in height and flightless. Brownie spirits are most often derived from acorns, pinecones, river stones, mosses, clover, or mushrooms. They like to live with people and are usually helpful, but can wreak havoc if not properly rewarded with pastries and milk. Brownies delight in playing tricks on fairies. Ironically, brownies are the keepers of the Feather of Hope, which is the means by which all hope on Earth is

*replenished and distributed. Brownies
ride on birds and animals to travel
and carry out their job of spreading
hope. Brownies are never invited to
Fairy Circle!*

Beth showed her aunt the last line in the handbook, but didn't ask another question because Aunt Evelyn nodded and put a finger to her lips.

Madam Toad waited until the noise had died down completely and all attention was again focused on her before going on. "Something terrible has happened, and the brownies need our help." With this she turned the meeting over to Brownie Christopher.

He stepped forward, cleared his throat, and kicked at a pebble. He looked a little older than Beth, maybe twelve or thirteen. Beth thought he was rather a handsome boy, even if he *was* full of mischief. When he spoke, his voice was deeper than she expected. "The brownies no longer have the Feather of Hope."

After waiting for the gasps of the fairies to subside, he explained further. "Three days ago, current keeper of the feather, Brownie Matthew, made a terrible mistake. He left it unattended briefly while orchestrating a prank. When he returned to the feather, it had been taken." Christopher paused to let this information sink in, then continued. "Matthew feels terrible about this. He has been permanently relieved of feather duty. He is also on prank restriction for an entire year. But it is very important that we get the feather back quickly. Already, hope is running thin."

Christopher shuffled his feet again and stuffed his hands into his pockets before going on. "A man named Mr. Forrester picked up the feather. He is currently using it as a bookmark. Mr. Forrester collects things like leaves, acorns, and feathers so it is understandable why he picked it up. Ordinarily, it would not be a problem for a brownie to retrieve it. Mr. Forrester works nights so the mission would be a safe and quiet one. However, Mr. Forrester is a very unlucky man. His house is inhabited by gremlins." As more gasps and murmurs broke out, Christopher paused again, and Beth looked up gremlins in her handbook.

> *Gremlins:* Nasty earth spirits who are invisible to regular human beings. They seek out unlucky people and dwell in their homes, garages, sheds, or offices. The gremlins' sole purpose in life is to break machines, appliances, and other mechanical devices. Gremlins are very mean. They have sharp teeth and claws, move very fast, and can hurt fairies. Be careful.

Beth could hear many fairies complaining loudly. "Brownies can never be trusted!" "Irresponsible!" "This is terrible!" "Why was the feather entrusted to them in the first place?"

As the noise grew, Madam Toad took matters into her own hands. "Calm! Everyone, stay calm!" Instantly there was silence, and Madam Toad said, "Let's discuss this reasonably. Gremlins are very dangerous to fairies and brownies. But there are three things that gremlins are afraid of: stainless steel, vacuum cleaners, and dachshunds. Please gather in small groups to brainstorm possible solutions to this problem."

Beth and Aunt Evelyn gathered with Thistle, Dragonfly, Firefly, and their mentors. Thistle immediately asked a question. "Why hasn't Mr. Forrester just gotten rid of the gremlins with his vacuum cleaner?"

Dragonfly quickly responded with the answer. "Because he can't see them.

Gremlins are invisible to regular people. Besides, his vacuum cleaner is probably broken by now." After a moment's thought, she added, "And a lot of people don't have enough stainless steel in their homes. They either can't afford it, or don't know that it's a worthwhile investment. Mr. Forrester must not have much in his home, or the gremlins wouldn't have moved in."

"You seem to know a lot about stainless steel, Jennifer," Firefly observed.

"Well, my mom's a dentist, so she's pretty keen on it. Pretty unlucky for Mr. Forrester not to have much."

"Maybe he's just unlucky to begin with..." countered Thistle.

"People make their own luck," Dragonfly interrupted sharply.

Firefly sighed and added, "So that just leaves dachshunds."

A few seconds later, all eyes turned to Beth who had exclaimed loudly, "Oh!" She

...but there are three things that gremlins are afraid of...

was looking positively ready to explode, and with a glance at Aunt Evelyn's smiling, knowing face, she took a deep breath and said excitedly, "Peanut!"

"This is no time for a snack, Marigold," Thistle said impatiently.

"No, No. I mean my dog, Peanut. He's a dachshund," Beth explained. She had a perfect picture in her mind of the last time she saw Peanut. He was lying on his yellow floor cushion next to Beth's bed, playing with his favorite squeaky toy shaped like a

Peanut

hot dog. Beth had petted him good-bye before dragging her suitcase downstairs to wait for Aunt Evelyn. "I'm sure he would be willing to help," Beth added.

Within a few minutes, they had a plan. Beth and Aunt Evelyn approached Madam Toad, who was even more impressive close up. Beth saw that she had a small crown of tiny miniature rosebuds to match her wand, and the pale green overskirt of her dress was shimmering with moisture drops. Beth could see her own golden reflection in Madam Toad's gigantic shining black eyes. Madam Robin moved closer to hear their conversation.

As they explained their plan, Christopher listened intently. For the first time, Beth noticed that he was not the only brownie at Fairy Circle. Two other brownies stood in the shadows behind Madam Toad, along with an owl, a squirrel, and a raven.

The other brownies were dressed similarly to Christopher in tans and browns. One had blond hair with a mossy green cap on his head and a spiral snail shell on a string slung across his back. The other had messy light brown hair stuffed under a hat that looked like a mushroom. They seemed to blend in with the tree trunk and shadows. Beth had only noticed them when they moved, shuffling their feet and stuffing their hands into their pockets.

Madam Toad cleared her throat, and with an attention-getting croak, she addressed the fairies. "I think we have a good plan. Marigold has a dachshund named Peanut who would be willing to help us. She and Madam Monarch will collect him and meet the brownies tomorrow night at Mr. Forrester's home. Madam Robin, Firefly, Dragonfly, and Thistle will also help.

"With this combination of fairy power, the mission should be successful. Unless anyone has a better plan, we will conclude our meeting and wait for news of the feather rescue."

She paused a moment for anyone to give further input or ideas, but there was silence. Most of the fairies were beaming in admiration at Beth and Aunt Evelyn, obviously impressed, and some were looking very relieved not to have to face the gremlins themselves.

Christopher approached Beth and said curtly, "We will meet you tomorrow night at nine." With a final nod to Madam Toad, he turned to leave, climbing onto the owl. His companions swung themselves onto the backs of the squirrel and raven. Within seconds they were gone.

Madam Toad chuckled and announced, "That is the first time brownies have ever been in company with fairies without pulling a prank. I never thought I'd live to see it."

Several fairies were already turning to leave when Dragonfly approached Madam Toad. "I have a complaint," she said angrily. Pointing to the fire, she continued. "Why didn't you bring a fire shield? I would have brought one myself if I had known. It's not any bigger than a coin. You have permanently scarred the earth and this stone." Beth looked closely. The fire was only about one inch wide and the stone Dragonfly referred to was a small pebble that was scorched on one side.

Madam Toad gave a small flick of her wand, which extinguished the fire. Then with a further wave of the rosebud stem, the black earth turned brown again, and the burned area on the rock lightened. There was only a small trace of gray where the scorch had been.

Dragonfly stamped her foot. "It doesn't matter that we can fix it. If we aren't diligent, apathy and carelessness will take over. What kind of example are we setting? 'Leave only footprints' is supposed to be our motto."

Madam Toad gazed calmly at Dragonfly, then stated, "Quite right, dear. Next time, please bring your fire shield." With that, Madam Toad turned to speak to a yellow rose fairy, and Dragonfly went back to join Thistle and Firefly.

Beth gazed breathlessly at Dragonfly as she passed, and uttered, "Wow, she's perfect."

"No, she isn't," Aunt Evelyn said quickly. She looked sharply at Beth. "If you mean that she is graceful, accomplished, intelligent, strong, principled, beautiful, and a natural leader, then yes, she is very nearly perfect. But she is also impulsive and quick to judge others. And she will need to learn to control her temper," she added firmly.

They walked back to their group to finalize plans for the mission.

Chapter Six

Feather Rescue

After several long discussions the next day about fairies, brownies, and gremlins, Beth and her aunt set out to collect Peanut late in the afternoon. Driving the back roads and byways gave them plenty more time to talk. Aunt Evelyn laughed merrily at Beth's latest question: "Are freckles really fairy kisses?"

"No, but I can tell you that the more freckles a fairy has, the more powerful she is, that's for sure." Aunt Evelyn's eyes were twinkling, and Beth wasn't sure if she was serious.

"Now remember the plan," Aunt Evelyn said as they approached Beth's house. "I'll distract your mother and tell her we've come to get your skates. Remember to be in fairy form when you talk to Peanut, so he'll understand you. In fairy form, your voice is the right pitch and tone to speak clearly to animals. And remember to actually get the skates."

Beth gave her mother a quick hug and ran upstairs. She could just hear Aunt Evelyn saying, "Oh yes, I got a brand-new pair of Rollerblades on sale, and Bethy promised to teach me some moves."

After a quick fairy discussion with the extremely eager Peanut, Beth was out the back door, carrying her skates and dog in her arms. She ran around front to Aunt Evelyn's car and deposited them both in the back seat, warning Peanut, "Stay down until we drive away." He nodded, panting, his tail wagging furiously. Aunt Evelyn appeared a few moments later and they set off.

They spent the rest of the afternoon explaining the feather rescue plan more thoroughly to Peanut. Then they ate dinner, watching Maximillion and Peanut bat around a tennis ball in the living room.

They set off a little after eight to meet the other fairies early and to go over the plan before the brownies arrived. Mr. Forrester lived on Bloomsbury Boulevard. Aunt Evelyn's lime green car rolled to a stop outside his gate just as the sun was going down. Thistle, Dragonfly, Firefly, and Madam Robin flew in within minutes. Aunt Evelyn and Beth changed into fairy form and followed Peanut around to the back door. He sat quietly waiting by the steps while the fairies perched on a window ledge. Gazing inside, they sighted three of Mr. Forrester's gremlins.

Beth was a little shocked—and afraid— at her first sight of gremlins. Two of them were on the couch, and one of them was

standing on a lamp table, fiddling with the wiring of the lamp. The two on the couch were just sitting and twiddling their gnarled thumbs. One was hissing at the other his wish that Mr. Forrester would come home tonight with some new appliance for them to break.

The gremlins looked to be about a foot high, and were a grayish, green-black color with tufts of coarse hair sticking out of their large, pointy ears. They were ugly, lumpy creatures with knobby hands and feet, long claws, sharp yellow teeth, and bulging eyes. Beth thought it was very good that regular people couldn't see gremlins, or they would be terrified.

Beth looked as scared as she felt. She glanced down worriedly at Peanut, who was patiently watching them with his glittering brown eyes. His cinnamon coat shone in the moonlight, and his ears fluttered a little with the night breezes.

Aunt Evelyn seemed to know what Beth was thinking because she said quietly, "Don't worry, Beth, Peanut knows how to handle a gremlin." As if in answer to this, Peanut wagged his tail and turned around to sit facing the door. He became very still and attentive, as though getting ready.

The brownies arrived and Christopher introduced the other two who had been at Fairy Circle. The blond, moss-capped brownie was Joel and the messy-haired, mushroom brownie was Alan.

After the awkward introductions in which the fairies blushed and the brownies shuffled their feet, Aunt Evelyn began going over safety rules. "Gremlins can jump about four feet, so stay high enough to be clear. The brownies won't go in until Peanut has cleared out all the gremlins. Christopher and Alan have been studying the house and have spied six gremlins in residence. Madam Robin will keep watch and let us know when all of them are out. Everyone stay in fairy form. I will transform long enough to prop the door open." She paused before asking, "Is everyone ready?"

Aunt Evelyn hovered near the lock of the back door and gave a small wave of her dandelion seed wand. A glittering stream of green light shot out and with a loud *click* the door was unlocked. She transformed just long enough to prop the door open with a brick.

Peanut needed no urging. He streaked through the door immediately, his paws racing along the carpet. Ignoring the gremlins in the living room, he headed straight for the back of the house to start in the farthest room and work his way forward. The three gremlins he passed had terrified and surprised looks on their faces.

Firefly lit the way and the fairies streamed into the house. Marigold and Thistle had to rise almost to the ceiling to avoid a lunging jump from the gremlin on the lamp table. Dragonfly zoomed quickly around his head to distract him.

The other two gremlins took up the fight, climbing onto the back of the couch and jumping as high as they could to try to reach the fairies. Thistle managed to poke one of them in the shoulder with her porcupine quill. And Aunt Evelyn's dandelion seed wand sent orange sparks flying to

sting the gremlins' noses. Beth just tried to stay out of everyone's way and hovered close to Firefly, who was focused on glowing as brightly as possible to light the room.

The gremlins were more furious than ever. Their sharp teeth gnashed and they jumped even higher to try to reach the fairies. And the hairs in their ears seemed to be snapping with electricity as they shouted, *"Blasted fairies!"*

After several minutes, Peanut arrived, panting and growling. He had managed to route the other three gremlins into the living room. The six gremlins seemed to take heart in their numbers for a moment because they laughed and began a frenzy of jumping and snarling at the fairies and at Peanut. But Peanut stood his ground. He circled them, herding them toward the back door.

One particularly vicious gremlin started throwing things at the fairies. Dragonfly dodged a book and flew straight at him. She landed on the gremlin's head and gave his left ear a hard walloping kick that was reminiscent of one of her best soccer moves. The gremlin howled in pain but was unable to reach her as she quickly zoomed away.

Aunt Evelyn's voice boomed as she stung another gremlin with her wand. "Out! Out I say! This dachshund is no weakling! And I will stay here all night stinging you if necessary!"

The gremlins snarled and snapped, but Peanut continued to growl and circle. Finally, all six gremlins gave up, and tripping over each other, they flooded out the back door. Aunt Evelyn followed and waited for the sharp, singing voice of Madam Robin to announce, "All clear!" from her post on the back fence.

The fairies landed around Peanut, giving him hugs and pats while he wriggled happily. He sat proudly watching, while the fairies set out to finish their work. Aunt Evelyn returned, leading the brownies. Alan, Joel, and Christopher immediately went to Mr. Forrester's tall bookcase and began to climb. When the boys reached the third shelf, they pulled out a book. The fairies gathered around to watch. None of them had ever seen the Feather of Hope before.

The book turned out to be Mr. Forrester's journal. Alan opened the book to the place marked by the feather. The feather was simply a small pure white feather, about three inches long, with no fancy markings or lacy frills. Despite its lack of impressiveness, the feather was obviously very powerful. Almost immediately a pleasant rush of feelings filled the room, like Christmas and Easter happening at the same time. They had delightful thoughts of babies laughing, finding treasure, and the smell of freshly baked cookies. Hope and happiness spread through the group. Even the brownies were smiling.

Looking at the last journal entry, which had been marked by the feather, Firefly read aloud:

"Life. In our search for meaning, there are two important things to consider: how we treat other people, and what we teach to children."

No one said anything for a moment, then round-eyed and solemn, Thistle softly whispered, "Mr. Forrester may be unlucky, but he's brilliant."

The brownies left a bluebird feather in the journal to replace the Feather of Hope. Then they thanked the fairies and set off. A fox, an eagle, and a squirrel were waiting for them outside. Alan, the new keeper of the feather, mounted the eagle and immediately soared away to begin spreading hope. Christopher and Joel left a few moments later, thanking them one last time and waving as they rode off on the fox and squirrel. Madam Robin also left, waving good-bye with a little flutter of her wing.

The fairies went back inside Mr. Forrester's house. Beth watched, fascinated, as Thistle and Dragonfly sped around fixing things. Firefly provided the light for them. Beth started to help too, delighted to find out that she was able to fix things by sprinkling glittering pixie dust and uttering, "*Repair,*" as she flicked her wand.

For about thirty minutes they traveled around the house, seeking out broken appliances and mechanical devices. Then they returned to the door to report their progress to Aunt Evelyn. Thistle said breathlessly, "We fixed the toaster, blender, pencil sharpener, blow-dryer, television, vacuum cleaner, computer, coffee pot, alarm clock, and two lamps, but we can't figure out what's wrong with the microwave. Mr. Forrester will probably just need to get a new one."

As Aunt Evelyn closed and locked the back door, Dragonfly pulled out a newspaper clipping, which she slid into the crack by the doorknob. She explained, "They have dachshund puppies available for adoption at the pound. Maybe Mr. Forrester will get lucky."

The girls all felt very good about the success of the mission as they piled into the station wagon. Aunt Evelyn wanted to give everyone a ride home, since it was a little late for young fairies to be flying around by themselves.

Chapter Seven

Peanut's Treat

It was after eleven o'clock when Aunt Evelyn dropped Peanut off at home. He padded happily through the grass to the front door, nodding hello to Mr. Tibbons as he passed. Mr. Tibbons was the gnome who came every Thursday night, as part of his garden route, to check on the progress of Mrs. Parish's flowers and vegetables. He helped tend the garden and added colors as needed.

Of course, the only time Mrs. Parish had ever actually seen Mr. Tibbons, he looked just like a large purple eggplant to her. But Peanut could see him as a gnome. Pulling a

Mr. Tibbons
the Garden Gnome

bit of crabgrass, Mr. Tibbons smiled and waved a dirty hand at Peanut.

Peanut scratched a little on the front door, wondering if Mr. or Mrs. Parish would be up this late to let him in. If not, he would just have to sleep on the front steps.

Mrs. Parish was indeed up, and was very upset. "Where have you been?" she demanded. "Out wandering around doing who knows what. I was so worried. You're lucky the pound didn't pick you up. You're lucky a car didn't run you over. What have you been doing all this time? Go straight upstairs! No supper for you!" Mrs. Parish finally finished her tirade, flushed and out of breath, and pointed to the stairs.

Peanut went straight up to Beth's room, his toenails clicking on the hardwood floor. He was sorry about missing dinner, but he felt very good about himself. He had helped to rescue the Feather of Hope, so even though he was tired and hungry, he couldn't be sad.

He had barely settled on his cushion and given his hot dog toy a squeaky squeeze goodnight when he heard a noise. Peanut was surprised to see Brownie Joel raising the window. There was a blueberry muffin slung across his back. He presented the muffin to Peanut, saying, "Thanks for your help today." Joel left quickly, smiling at the astonished dachshund. Peanut joyously wolfed down the muffin in three bites and returned to his floor pillow, very satisfied.

But it wasn't time for sleep yet. Mrs. Parish arrived in the doorway two minutes later, sliding Peanut's dog food bowl inside the room. *My kibbles!* thought Peanut happily. He ran to the dish and ate his supper quickly. Ten minutes later, before he finally drifted off to sleep, he thought about what was probably the best day of his life. He had helped the fairies carry out important work, and it was the first and only time he ever had a dessert before his meal.

Three houses down the block from the
Parish home, Mrs. Gurnsky was frantically
searching for the blueberry muffin she had
set out for a snack before going to roll her
hair. She was positive it had been right
beside her cup of chamomile tea. This was
certainly a mystery.

Next door to Mrs. Gurnsky, Mr. Porter
wasn't worried about tea or muffins. He
had just been to see his wife in the hospital.

For several days, he had been in despair, thinking she was nearing the end. But tonight, at around ten o'clock, he had felt a strong surge of hope that she might get well. Tonight he would sleep peacefully, without being wakened by worry.

Chapter Eight

Nut Messages
and One More Adventure

Beth woke the next morning feeling very alive and happy. Eating bacon, eggs, and toast, she talked excitedly to Aunt Evelyn about their first fairy adventure. After breakfast, Aunt Evelyn suggested they check to see if there were any messages from the other fairies.

"How do fairies send messages to each other?" Beth asked.

"We use nut messaging by means of birds and small animals," Aunt Evelyn replied. "In fact, I'd be very surprised if there weren't already some messages for you upstairs."

They went up to Beth's room and walked
over to the open window. Sure enough, on the
windowsill sat two acorns and a pecan. They
looked just like ordinary nuts. Aunt Evelyn
gathered them and placed them on the bed,
instructing Beth to change into fairy form.
With two small *pops*, Beth and Aunt Evelyn
were sitting on the bumpy blue bedspread.

Looking closely with her tiny fairy eyes,
Beth could see a small clasp on each of the
nuts. She opened the lids of the hollow nut

containers, revealing small pieces of paper, which were messages from her new fairy friends. One of the acorns also contained a lemon jellybean, and Aunt Evelyn explained, "All fairies like lemon jellybeans; we're just mad about them."

Beth read Firefly's message first.

I'm so glad I got to meet you. Thank you for your help last night. And please thank Peanut too. He was fantastic. I wish Mom and Dad would let me have a dog.
See you next week,
Lenox

Thistle wrote:

Wow Beth! You and Peanut are really a great team. Thanks for your help. By the way, I think Brownie Alan likes you. He asked me about you. But we can talk more about him when I see you next.
Bye for now,
Grace

And finally, Dragonfly's message read:

It was great working with you. I hear you are going to be at Camp Hopi the last week of July. I'll be there too. Let's see if we can sign up to be tentmates.

See you Tuesday,

Jennifer

Beth was very excited about the messages, but she was confused. She asked her aunt, "What's happening next week? Another Fairy Circle?"

Aunt Evelyn smiled and replied, "I was saving it as a surprise, but I suppose I will have to tell you now. We are going to help Madam Tooth Fairy next Tuesday night. She is having dental work that day and won't be able to fly that evening. We will be taking over her duties for her."

Over the next few days, Beth ate loads of lemon jellybeans and happily sent and received nut messages. Doves, mockingbirds, and hummingbirds in the back yard were all more than happy to deliver the nuts. As news of their success in the feather rescue spread, she and Aunt Evelyn both got messages from other fairies, congratulating them. Beth even received a small gift of a friendship bracelet from a carnation fairy named Wendy that she had never met.

While Beth was writing out messages, a large grackle delivered a walnut to the windowsill. When Beth opened it, a puffy gray plant pod exploded in her face, showering her with smelly, sooty powder. Included with the stink bomb was a message from Alan:

> *Hope to see you again sometime.*
>
> *Thanks for your help,*
>
> *Alan*

Beth decided not to get upset about the prank. After all, she reasoned, brownies really couldn't help themselves when it came to mischief. And remembering that brownies like pastries, Beth sent the walnut back with a bit of a chocolate éclair stuffed inside. Keeping on good terms with the brownies seemed like a good idea, especially since Thistle had said that Alan liked her.

On Tuesday, about twenty fairies met at the Tooth Fairy's house. Along with Thistle, Dragonfly, and Firefly, Beth recognized Spiderwort and Rosemary. She finally got to meet Wendy, the carnation fairy, and thank her for the bracelet. She also got to talk to several other fairies,

including Tulip, Magnolia, Periwinkle, Lily, and Primrose.

They had a wonderful time working in pairs with little bags of dimes and small pouches to collect the teeth. Madam Tooth Fairy explained that fairies didn't need to carry anything larger than dimes, and that parents could add to that amount if they wanted to.

For several hours, fairies flitted in and out of the house emptying pouches, picking up more dimes, and checking addresses of children who had lost teeth that day. Aunt Evelyn kept company with Madam Tooth Fairy, making tea and helping refill a hot water bottle to soothe the ache in her cheek from her dental work that day.

The next day, Beth found out something that was almost as amazing as being a fairy. Aunt Evelyn actually did own a pair of Rollerblades. They spent the whole morning skating up and down Cherry Lane and talking about fairy things.

On Friday, with Aunt Evelyn's permission, Beth took a fairy field trip with Firefly, Dragonfly, and Thistle. They flew together to Mr. Forrester's house on Bloomsbury Boulevard.

Mr. Forrester had indeed adopted a dachshund puppy from the pound, had named him Lucky, and was training him in the back yard. The fairies were delighted and sat watching in the shade of a rosebush while Lucky practiced sitting and heeling.

After a few minutes, Mr. Forrester and Lucky took a break to play fetch with a rolled-up sock. The fairies flew away with a last look at Lucky, who was barking happily, his ears flying as he chased the sock.

When she left Aunt Evelyn's house at the end of her two-week visit, Beth thought it was the best summer she had ever had. And she still had camp to look forward to.

With a last look at Aunt Evelyn's house as they were leaving, Beth realized that all of the mixed-up colors of the house were perfect, just like the colors in nature. And Aunt Evelyn had never looked more beautiful in a bright pink dress with a wide green sash and a light blue straw hat perched on her head. In fact, she looked like a tall, leafy pink flower that was touching the sky.

As she dropped Beth off at home, Aunt Evelyn gave her a final bit of advice. "Now that you know you are a fairy, be careful of jigsaw puzzles. Fairies can get lost in them." Aunt Evelyn gave a little shiver, adding, "All those curving lines." Beth waved to Aunt Evelyn as she drove off, and went inside to hug her parents and Peanut, and to look up jigsaw puzzles in her handbook.

The End

Fairy Fun

Powdered Sugar Puff Pastries Recipe

300° 15 min.

(Courtesy of Madam June Beetle)

2 C. flour

1 T. baking powder

1 C. real butter (softened)

1/2 C. powdered sugar

2 t. lemon extract (or raspberry, orange, etc.)

2 T. water

1 C. extra powdered sugar in separate bowl to coat cookies after baking

Mix flour and baking powder together. In separate bowl, cream butter and sugar together. Add lemon extract and water. Add flour mixture and combine well.

With your fingers, form into 3/4 inch balls and place on an ungreased cookie sheet 2 inches apart. Bake at 300° for 15 min. While still warm, coat with powdered sugar. Serve warm, room temperature, or refrigerated.

For a chocolate mint version: use peppermint extract and add 1 T. cocoa powder to the flour mixture.

Be sure to get permission from your parents to cook in the kitchen, and make sure a grown-up helps when using sharp instruments and hot appliances.

FAIRY FACTS

Pussy Willows

Pussy willow stems come from pussy willow trees. The trees grow mainly in Canada and in the Eastern United States. The furry buds on the branches are called catkins, but are sometimes nicknamed pussy toes. The size of the trees can vary greatly, generally anywhere from three to twenty feet. Pussy willows grow in the wetlands and need a goodly amount of rain, but they also like a lot of sun.

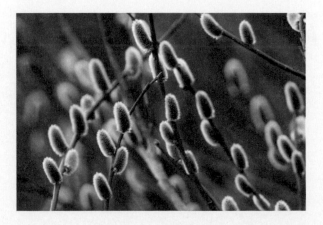

Monarch Butterflies

Monarch butterflies lay their eggs on the leaves of milkweed plants. When the larvae hatch, they eat the leaves. This milkweed plant diet provides toxins to give the butterflies protection against predators such as birds and lizards. The monarchs must migrate south from their northern homes in Canada each year because they cannot survive in cold temperatures.

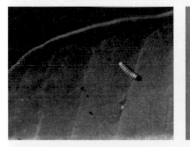 

Monarch butterflies are the only butterflies in the world that make such a lengthy migration. Eastern populations of monarchs winter in Mexico. Those west of the Rocky Mountains winter in California. It takes several generations of monarchs to make the full migration, and it is a great mystery as to how the same families of monarch butterflies return to the same winter nesting spots each year.

Cottingley Fairies

In 1918, in England, two young girls, Frances Griffiths and Elsie Wright, took pictures of themselves with fairies they said they had found in the gardens around Cottingley. You can see a few of the fairies in these pictures. They became known as Cottingley Fairies. Tales of the fairies spread all over England, and soon people were flocking to come see the fairies, though no one seemed to be able to see them, or capture them on film, except for Frances and Elsie. Even the author of *Sherlock Holmes*, Sir Arthur Conan Doyle, was convinced that they existed and even wrote a

story about them. It took many years, but in 1982, nearly seventy years after the photos were taken, the young girls, now old ladies, admitted that the photographs had been faked. But still, every year many people travel to Cottingley, some just to see the famous gardens, but some with the secret hope that even though the photographs are fake, the fairies might still be real.

Inside you is the power to do anything

The Fairy Chronicles

. . . the adventures continue

Dragonfly and the Web of Dreams

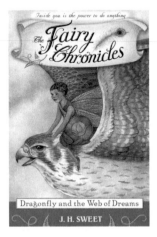

Dragonfly and the Web of Dreams

J. H. SWEET

Dragonfly and her closest friends, Marigold, Thistle, and Firefly have all been having terrible nightmares all week long. So it comes as no surprise that the problem is getting worse, and not just for fairies. An emergency Fairy Circle is called...

"Welcome, welcome! Attention, attention everyone! We are here to discuss the problem of the nightmares. First of all, we need to thank the doves."

Madam Toad gestured to one side of the gathering where several tired and bedraggled looking doves were cooing sleepily. "They have been working overtime, delivering good dreams to help balance out the dream problem. It would be much worse if not for their efforts."

There was polite applause and Madam Toad continued. "The Web of Dreams has been destroyed. I went with the Sandman yesterday to confirm this. It is not clear who destroyed it or how anyone knew its location. But it must be rebuilt quickly or the problem will worsen."

The fairy team must find the Dream Spider, discover the cause of the Web's destruction, and get a new one built before the whole world succumbs to nightmares and good dreams become a thing of the past.

Now Available in Bookstores and Online

Thistle and the Shell of Laughter

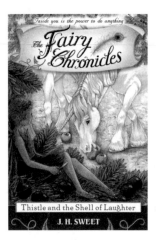

The Shell of Laughter has been stolen from Staid, the Elf! Madam Toad sends Thistle and her friends to recapture the Shell and return it to its rightful place before all laughter is lost forever. But a very dangerous enemy has control of the Shell.

Killjoy Crosspatch, the Spirit of Sorrow, stared at them without speaking. Thistle, Marigold, and Dragonfly thought he was the most disgusting and foul creature they had ever seen. "Where is the shell?" demanded Staid.

Killjoy Crosspatch didn't speak. Instead, a wide, uneven smile crept across his ugly face, and he slowly raised his hands in front of him. From his dripping palms, a dark gray, smoky cloud began to seep. It slowly crept towards the elf, the hedgehog, the leprechaun, Madam Robin, and the fairies.

They tried to take cover behind several of the rocks, but the oozing darkness followed them. It seemed there was no escape from the cloud of sorrow.

Can they do it? Will the fairies defeat the Spirit of Sorrow and return the Shell to its rightful owner? More important, will the world ever get to laugh again?

Coming in July 2007

Firefly and the Quest of the Black Squirrel

Firefly and the Quest of the Black Squirrel

J. H. SWEET

Firefly and her friends are going on a camping trip. But little do they know that they are about to be sent on a real adventure, where the stakes are nothing less than the future of all the species on Earth.

The black squirrel looked nervous. When he spoke, his soft voice quavered a little at first. "I have made a long journey to be here because a terrible sickness has struck several black squirrel colonies in the far North, and it is spreading. The sickness causes death."

The black squirrel stopped his story for a moment. When he started speaking again, his voice shook. "But I haven't told you the worst part. The curse is a *Calendar-Chain-Curse,* set up to attack a new species each month. Next month, all white-tailed deer will die. In May, beavers, and the following month, earthworms. In July, snow geese, and so on. Eventually, it will reach humans. There is no stopping it." He sighed, "It is a *perfect curse.*"

This is a very dangerous mission and Madam Toad is dispatching some of her best fairies for this mission: Firefly, Thistle, Marigold, and their new friend Periwinkle. The girls will have to use all of their magic, brains, and brawn to stop the perfect curse!

Coming in July 2007

About the Author

J.H. Sweet has always looked for the magic in the everyday. She has an imaginary dog named Jellybean Ebenezer Beast. Her hobbies include hiking, photography, knitting, and basketry. She also enjoys watching a variety of movies and sports. Her favorite superhero is her husband, with Silver Surfer coming in a close second. She loves many of the same things the fairies love, including live oak trees, mockingbirds, weathered terra-cotta, butterflies, bees, and cypress knees. In the fairy game of "If I were a jellybean, what flavor would I be?" she would be green apple. J.H. Sweet lives with her husband in South Texas and has a degree in English from Texas State University.

About the Illustrator

Ever since she was a little girl, Tara Larsen Chang has been captivated by intricate illustrations in fairy tales and children's books. Since earning her BFA in Illustration from Brigham Young University, her illustrations have appeared in numerous children's books and magazines. When she is not drawing and painting in her studio, she can be found working in her gardens to make sure that there are plenty of havens for visiting fairies.